PUFFIN BOOKS

DANCING SHOES
FRIENDS AND RIVALS

Antonia Barber was born in London and grew up in Sussex. While studying English at London University, she spent her evenings at the Royal Opera House, where her father worked, watching the ballet and meeting many famous dancers. She married a fellow student and lived in New York before settling back in England. She has three children, including a daughter who did ballet from the age of three and attended the Royal Ballet School Junior Classes at Sadler's Wells.

Her best-known books are *The Ghosts*, which was runner-up for the Carnegie Medal and was filmed as *The Amazing Mr Blunden*, and *The Mousehole Cat*.

Antonia lives in an old oast house in Kent and a little fisherman's cottage in Cornwall.

If you like dancing and making friends, you'll love

DANCING SHOES

Lucy Lambert – Lou to her friends – dreams of one day becoming a great ballerina. Find out if Lucy's dream comes true in:

DANCING SHOES: LESSONS FOR LUCY
DANCING SHOES: INTO THE SPOTLIGHT
DANCING SHOES: LUCY'S NEXT STEP
(available October 1998)

And look out for more DANCING SHOES titles coming soon

Antonia Barber

DANCING SHOES
Friends and Rivals

Illustrated by Biz Hull

AlisonMacrae

PUFFIN BOOKS

PUFFIN BOOKS

Published by the Penguin Group
Penguin Books Ltd, 27 Wrights Lane, London W8 5TZ, England
Penguin Putnam Inc., 375 Hudson Street, New York, New York 10014, USA
Penguin Books Australia Ltd, Ringwood, Victoria, Australia
Penguin Books Canada Ltd, 10 Alcorn Avenue, Toronto, Ontario, Canada M4V 3B2
Penguin Books (NZ) Ltd, 182–190 Wairau Road, Auckland 10, New Zealand

Penguin Books Ltd, Registered Offices: Harmondsworth, Middlesex, England

First published 1998
1 3 5 7 9 10 8 6 4 2

Typeset in 15/22 Monotype Calisto

Made and printed in England by Clays Ltd, St Ives plc

British Library Cataloguing in Publication Data
A CIP catalogue record for this book is available from the British Library

ISBN 0–140–38684–X

Chapter One

Lou stood on the corner of the street waiting for Emma. She shivered and pulled her coat closer around her. There was a cold wind blowing which was making her nose red. The snow, so white and magical a week before, was now grey with city dirt. It was melting fast, clogging the gutters and making puddles across the pavements. Lou's feet were freezing. She wished she could hurry on to the warm changing room but she had promised to meet Emma on the corner after school so that they could arrive at the Maple School of Ballet together. It was their first lesson in the new class and it was not going to be easy.

The Brownes' estate car pulled up sharply at the corner, showering icy water over Lou's feet. The door flew open and a pink and flustered Emma jumped out.

'I'm sorry, Lou, I couldn't find my ballet

bag. Someone had put it on the wrong peg. Are we very late?'

Lou waved to Mrs Browne as the big car pulled away from the kerb. 'It's OK,' she said, 'but we'd better get a move on.'

'Will they give us a bad time?' asked Emma as they hurried along the street.

'Sure to,' said Lou gloomily. 'You know what Angela is like.'

Emma knew only too well. She went to school with Angela, who was the most powerful girl in her class. If you didn't belong to Angela's group you were nobody, and she chose to leave Emma out. Even Lou had no idea how lonely Emma was, though she knew that her friend was not happy. They both wished they could go to the same school, but the Brownes sent their daughter to a private school while Lou's mother sent her to the local primary.

'I wish we could stay on in Miss Ashton's ballet class,' said Emma wistfully.

'It was fun,' agreed Lou. They had both enjoyed their first term in the beginners' class, especially when they were chosen to take part in the local pantomime. 'But we've got to move on, Em, if we really want to be ballet dancers. We'll have to work hard to catch up with Angela and the others.'

Emma sighed.

They ran up the wide stone steps of the Maple School of Ballet and along the echoing hallway. At the door of the changing room they paused to get their courage up. As they did so, Lou sensed suddenly that something was different.

'Wait,' she said, catching at Emma's sleeve. 'Listen!'

The familiar sounds of the younger ones dressing and having their hair done had changed somehow. The usual squeaking had become a distinct giggling and the shrieks were more like little squeals of excitement.

'Something's up!' said Lou and she pushed open the door.

Inside the changing room it seemed that all eyes were being drawn towards the far end of the room.

'Oh!' said Lou.

'Oh, Lou!' said Emma.

In the corner with his back towards them, raising his arms to pull his sweatshirt over his head, was a BOY . . .

Lou and Emma knew perfectly well that there were men in ballets. They even knew, if they thought about it, that these dancers must have had lessons when they were young. But they had never seen a boy at the Maple School of Ballet and they could not imagine any of the boys they knew going to ballet classes. Boys played football; they slouched about in sloppy clothes. They did not pull on tights and do *pliés*! Any boy who did that would be the biggest wimp in the world . . .

But then the Boy turned round and he didn't look at all wimpish. He was tall but not too thin, with smiley eyes and dark curly hair. Lou and Emma stared like all the others.

The Boy made his way through the

crush with his head lowered as if to avoid looking at the girls. As he reached the doorway he looked up and caught Lou's eye. He raised one eyebrow and grinned ruefully. Before she could recover and grin back, he had gone, followed by Angela and her friends in a breathless excited rush.

'Quick!' said Lou. 'Or we'll be the last.' She could not bear to think of the Boy talking to the simpering Angela.

But when they reached the studio, they found all the girls posing elegantly, while the Boy chatted to the elderly pianist.

Mrs Dennison followed them in and the class began. She put the three newcomers at the back, which gave Lou a chance to return the Boy's grin. She wondered if he would speak to her at the end of the class, but Mrs Dennison asked him to stay behind. She said Miss Maple wanted to see him. In the changing room the girls talked of nothing else.

'We needn't have worried,' said Emma as they walked home. 'I mean, Angela and her friends didn't make fun of us at all.'

Lou laughed. 'They didn't even notice *us*,' she said. 'That boy came in really useful.'

'He was nice, wasn't he?' said Emma.

'He wasn't just *nice*,' said Lou. 'He was . . . he was . . .' She couldn't find the right word to describe him. Then, shivering in the cold wind, she said at last, 'He was really special!'

Chapter Two

Melanie Jackson summed it up for the
girls at the local junior school. 'He is *so*
cool!' she said with the air of one who
knew about these things.

'Nice face,' said Liza Tompkins.

'And clever with it!' said Tracey Gibbs.

Lucy listened but said nothing. She had
not yet recovered from the shock of
finding that the Boy actually went to her
school.

'I bet he does gymnastics,' said Melanie. 'You can tell by the way he moves.'

'You only hope!' said Liza. 'Just because you do gym.'

'He does ballet,' said Lou, finding her voice for the first time.

'Ballet!'

'Boys don't do ballet!'

'You're joking!'

'Rudolf Nureyev did.'

'That's different. I mean boys from *our* school don't.'

'Well, this one does,' said Lou, 'because he goes to my ballet class . . . and he's pretty good too.'

Now she was the centre of attention.

'Does he wear tights?' (*giggle, giggle*)

'Did you talk to him?'

'What did he say?'

Lou did not want to admit that she had not spoken to him so she said, 'Oh, you know, this and that.'

She could see that her popularity had risen by several notches.

Walking home from school, they saw the Boy behind them, one of a group on bicycles, weaving lazily along the edge of the kerb. The girls raised their voices and kept looking round . . . Lou found it rather embarrassing. She had the longest walk home, and one by one her friends went their separate ways. When she was alone, she did look back and saw the Boy a little way behind. He caught her up, got off his bike and said, 'Hi! It's Lucy, isn't it?'

'Lou.' Her mouth went dry.

'I'm Jerome . . . after the songwriter, not the saint. My friends call me Jem.'

'Why were you named after a songwriter?'

'Because my gran is a Jerome Kern fan.'

'Who's he?' asked Lou.

'Oh, some famous songwriter. My gran also likes one called Cole Porter and another called Irving Berlin, so it could have been worse.'

'Your friends would have called you "Irv",' said Lou. They both made sick noises.

'Or Old King Cole?' he suggested.

'Even worse,' said Lou.

There was a silence while she tried to think of something sparkling to say. As they turned into her street a cold wind whipped them so she said, 'My mum makes hot chocolate when I get in. Would you like some?'

'Oh, great!' said Jem.

Lou had never brought a boy home before. He chained his bike to the railings while she opened the door. 'Hi, Mum!' she called. 'Hello, Soggybottom!'

'Not 'Bottom!' said Charlie indignantly, hugging her knee.

'Well, "Hi, Charlie" then.' Lou picked him up. 'My brother,' she explained to Jem and, as Jenny came out of the kitchen, she added, 'My mum.' To Jenny she said, 'This is Jem. He's new at school and he goes to our ballet class.' She wished she and Emma had not raved on about him so much the night before.

Jenny Lambert grinned. 'Brave lad!' she said. 'How do you cope with all those girls?'

'The changing room was a bit much,' said Jem, 'but Miss Maple says I can use the staff room.'

'Do the boys at school tease you?'

'They haven't found out yet. But I suppose they will . . . They did at my other school.'

'Did you mind?' asked Lou.

Jem shrugged. 'It was a pain,' he said, 'but I play a lot of football, so they decided I was OK.'

'Are you going to be a dancer?' asked

Lou. She had already altered her dream future to include him: a tall, curly-haired Nureyev standing by her side while she took her curtain calls.

'Don't really know. But I want to go to stage school and my gran says I'll need ballet to get in. My grandad is teaching me piano too.'

Lou wavered; maybe she would go to stage school too, instead of ballet school. But her dream of one day wearing a white-embroidered tutu was strong . . . and there was plenty of time to make Jem change his mind.

The door to the upstairs flat slammed and Emma came clattering down the stairs. She burst into the kitchen and stopped dead at the sight of Lou and Jem, side by side, drinking hot chocolate.

'Oh!' she said and turned rather pale.

'Hi!' said Lou. 'It's Jem . . . from the ballet class.'

'Yes,' said Emma. 'I can see.'

She did not look very happy; Lou thought maybe she was a bit jealous.

Jenny made some more hot chocolate.

'You're Emma, aren't you?' said Jem.

'Yes,' said Emma, brightening.

'You go to the same school as that Angela?'

'Yes,' said Emma darkening.

'Wow! What a girl!'

He realized suddenly that the warm kitchen had grown very frosty. Both girls were looking daggers at him and Lou's mum was making warning signals above their heads.

'Good ballet dancer, I mean,' he said hastily. 'Long legs . . . Dancers need long legs . . . I mean *strong* legs . . .'

They were still glaring at him.

He put down his mug and glanced at his watch. 'Gosh, is that the time?' he said. 'Well, I suppose I'd better be on my way . . . Thanks, Mrs Lambert . . .'

Chapter Three

Sometimes Lou felt cross with Jem and sometimes she felt cross with Emma. She knew this was not fair, but if Em had not come in when she did, Jem might never have mentioned Angela. And to make things worse, she did rather go on about it.

'I think he really likes Angela,' she would say.

'If he likes *her*, why did he walk home with me?'

'Well, Angela doesn't go to your school.'

'He could have walked with one of the other girls.'

'They don't go to the ballet class. Maybe he wanted to ask you about her . . .'

Lou was afraid she might be right, which made her even more cross.

The next night the boys had football practice and then it was the weekend. On Monday night Jem was nowhere to be seen. On Tuesday he rode behind Lou but did not try to catch up with her. She didn't look round. That night Lou had a serious talk with Emma.

'He'll be at ballet class tomorrow,' she said, 'and if we're horrid to him and

Angela is nice, he'll end up being her friend.'

'Well, yes . . . but . . .' Emma did not want to turn the twosome into a threesome. What if Lou became Jem's friend while she was left out? It was bad enough to have no friends at school, but if Jem took Lou away . . .

'Angela is vain enough now,' said Lou. 'If Jem is *her* friend she'll be impossible.'

'I suppose so . . .'

'And my mum says it's silly to be huffy just because he said . . .' Lou could not bring herself to repeat the offending words.

'Oh, well, in that case . . .' Emma thought very highly of Jenny Lambert's good sense.

*

Next evening in the changing room there was an air of deep gloom. The Boy was nowhere to be seen and all the little ones were moaning.

'It's all right,' Lou told them. 'He's changing in the staff room so he doesn't see all of you in your KNICKERS!'

The little ones giggled at the naughty word.

'How do *you* know?' asked one of Angela's friends.

'He told me on the way home the other night,' said Lou cheerfully. 'Didn't you know? He goes to my school.'

She swept out of the changing room with Emma, trailing clouds of glory.

Jem was already in the studio.

'Hi!' said Lou brightly. 'Haven't seen you all week.'

He seemed pleased that he was no longer in the doghouse.

'I did a lot of football practice,' he said.

'Do you like football?' asked Emma.

'Yeah, it's great!' His eyes lit up. 'I might be a footballer instead of going to stage school.'

Lou was shocked. He was going to be her personal Nureyev, not some stupid footballer.

Emma looked at him shyly. 'I might be

a teacher,' she confided. Lou glared at
her. Emma looked guilty. 'Of course, I'd
rather be a ballet dancer,' she said
quickly, 'but I'm not as good as you are,
Lou.'

'You could be a ballet teacher,' said
Jem, and Emma smiled at him gratefully.

Mrs Dennison arrived with the others
and the class swept into their graceful
révérences, all except Jem, who did an
elegant bow.

Lou wanted to watch him, so she stood
behind him at the *barre*. But Mrs
Dennison promptly changed them around
and left Lou knowing that he was
watching her. She did all her exercises as
beautifully as she could and Mrs
Dennison said, 'Well done, Lucy.'

But Lou was now standing behind

Angela and she could not help seeing that the fair girl was very good indeed. Her legs *were* long and seemed made for ballet. Her arms never seemed to have elbows sticking out, her head was gracefully poised on a slender neck. Lou

did not like her at all. She was mean to Emma and much too pleased with herself. I must keep Jem out of her clutches, she thought. She won't really want him for a friend, she'll just want to show him off.

'You are sticking your bottom out, Lucy,' called Mrs Dennison. 'Do keep your mind on your dancing!'

Now Lou felt really foolish and it was all Angela's fault!

As they hurried to change at the end of the lesson, Lou wondered if Jem would follow them home. She felt sure that he would . . . But as they came out on to the steps, a cold rain was falling and Mrs Browne was waiting to take them home in the car.

Chapter Four

On Saturday it was almost like spring. The wind dropped; the sun came out and the street market was crowded. The stall-holders breathed in the bright air and greeted their customers with a smile. Emma had abandoned her parents on their trip to the supermarket to go with Lucy and her mother. The girls were taking turns with Charlie's pushchair.

Mrs Dillon, the old lady who lived on

the top floor of the Brownes' house, had also joined the shopping party. Since Jenny Lambert had introduced her to the delights of the charity shops, she had been slowly changing her entire wardrobe. Each week her clothes grew more exotic. Lou and Emma were quite proud of her.

Now they rummaged together through piles of brilliant colour on a stall selling silk scarves. Lou could see Mrs Dillon eyeing the elegantly tied headscarf of a tall good-looking woman who lifted the bright silks with a slender, long-fingered hand. The woman laughed, turning to speak to the boy beside her, and Lou saw with a start that it was Jem. He looked up and grinned. 'What do you think, Lou? My gran can't decide between this

27

orangy-yellow one and that yellowy-orange.'

Lou couldn't see much difference but Mrs Dillon said firmly, 'This orangy-yellow is best. It is giving your lovely dark skin a rich glow.'

'Well, thank you . . .' The woman gave

Mrs Dillon a slow, charming smile. Lou thought she had never seen anyone so beautiful. She looked much too young to be Jem's grandmother.

A moment later he asked, 'Is that your gran?'

'Mrs Dillon?' said Lou, taken by surprise. 'No, she lives upstairs in our house and she helps us with our ballet practice.'

'She used to dance with the Bolshoi,' put in Emma. 'She was called Reena Brushover.'

'The Bolshoi! Wow!' Jem looked again at the old lady. 'You can see she's been on the stage. She's got that sort of style.'

Lou thought of Mrs Dillon when they had first met her – the dowdy brown frock and the sagging cardigan – but she only said, 'Your gran looks amazing too. Was she on the stage?'

'Still is,' said Jem. 'She's a singer and my grandad plays the clarinet. They met when they did a gig together.'

Lou began to see why he wanted to go to stage school and why he was not afraid to be seen in a ballet class. She was wishing her own family were more glamorous when she felt Emma jogging her elbow. She was trying to point out something behind Jem's back. Glancing over his shoulder, Lou saw Angela with her grandfather, looking at Indian jewellery on the next stall. Angela caught her eye and turned away. But Lou knew that she had seen them talking with Jem and that she was not pleased.

'Why are you both grinning like that?'

asked Jem. 'You look like a couple of cats who have been at the cream.'

'Oh, it's nothing,' said Lou airily.

'Nothing at all,' said Emma.

The women had moved on to a stall selling tropical vegetables, and Jem's gran was explaining to Lou's mum and Mrs Dillon how to cook some of the more unusual ones.

'You must come to us one day,' she said, smiling. 'Bring all the children. We will cook a Caribbean meal and play music together.'

Lou looked at Emma; Emma looked at Lou. They had been invited to Jem's house! Angela would be green with envy.

And then, 'How are my favourite Rats?' said a booming voice beside them.

They looked up to see Angela's

grandfather smiling down at them, while
Angela looked away and tried to pretend
they were not there. Lou and Emma liked
this fat, friendly man. They had met him
when they took part in the local dramatic
society's pantomime. He had played the
Merchant in *Dick Whittington* and Lou
and Emma had played
the Rats. Lou had
nicknamed him 'The

Wind-up Merchant' because he was always teasing them. The Rats grinned at him and said they were fine.

'You know my granddaughter Angela?' asked the Wind-up Merchant.

Lou and Emma said they did, but the girls did not speak to one another. The big man seemed disappointed.

'I hope you're both coming to Angela's party?' he said. 'Have you had your invitations?'

'Er . . . no . . .' said Lou.

Angela looked furious.

'They must be in the post,' said her grandfather. 'Saturday week . . . Mark it in your diaries.' And with that he moved on into the crowd, followed by Angela with her nose in the air.

'Was he winding us up again?' asked

Emma as they watched him go. 'I mean, Angela is never going to invite *us* to her party.'

'Maybe he was winding Angela up,' said Lou. 'You know what a tease he is!'

'What was all that about rats?' asked Jem, and they had to tell him about the pantomime.

'And will you go to her party . . . if you do get an invitation?' he asked.

Emma began to say, 'Well, if . . .' but Lou said firmly, 'She needn't worry. We wouldn't go to her rotten party if she paid us!'

'Ah, if only Angela would invite *me* to her party,' said Jem, rolling his eyes, 'I'd go like a shot!'

They both hit him.

Chapter Five

'Shoulders back, Emma. Raise your chin. You must stand tall and proud. A dancer must draw every eye towards her.' Mrs Dillon drew herself up and looked very superior. Emma tried to look the same.

'That is better. Do you not feel more confident?'

Emma sighed. People were always telling her to be more confident, so she tried to pretend that she was. She was not

even honest with Lou any more.
(*Arms into first position*
. . . look at hands
. . . left arm to second
position . . . look
right . . .) Lou
told her just
how to deal with
the girls at school
(*Right arm to*
second . . . look
over left arm . . .),
but when she got there, she couldn't do it.
And because she was ashamed of being
feeble, she pretended things were getting
better. (*Look to front . . . hands on waist . . .*)
But it wasn't true. (*Face front, third position,*
right foot in front . . .) If only Angela would
invite her to the party. (*Bend knees . . .*

demi plié . . . *three times . . .*) If just for
once, she could talk and laugh with the
other girls . . . (*Back to third, right foot
in front . . .*)

'Left foot, Emma,' said Mrs Dillon.
'Your mind is wandering.'

If they got to know her, they might
even like her . . . Lou liked her . . . Was
there an invitation in the post? If there
was, it would come tomorrow. But Lou
said that she wouldn't go even if she was
invited . . . and Emma knew that she
would never go without Lou.

At last Mrs Dillon said, 'That will do
now. You have been good girls. Now I go
and see if Charlie is still sleeping. Your
mother will be back from her evening
class soon.'

The girls did their *révérences* and then

flopped on to Emma's bed. They did their practice in Emma's room now because Mr Browne had fixed up a big mirror which he had found in a junk shop. It was a bit worn in places but it helped the girls to see their mistakes. He had also fitted a baby monitor so that Mrs Dillon could hear if Charlie woke up during their practice session.

There was a lot of noise and confusion in the Brownes' part of the house. Emma's father was refitting their kitchen.

'We'll have to watch on your video,' said Emma. 'Dad's drill makes our picture go all funny. It's like this every evening now. I wish he'd get a builder to do it while I'm at school.'

'Can't he get one?' asked Lou as they went downstairs. She thought Mr Browne must be able to afford a builder: he had an important job in a bank.

'He likes doing it,' Emma sighed. 'He says he'd rather be a carpenter than a banker.'

'So why doesn't he?'

'My granny wouldn't let him. She said she didn't pay a fortune for his schooling to have him be a carpenter.'

'Jesus was a carpenter,' Lou pointed out.

'That's what my dad said, but Granny said Jesus didn't have an expensive private education.'

Lou thought about it. Emma went to a private school. 'Will you have to be what your granny says?' she asked.

'I expect so,' said Emma gloomily.

'Will she let you be a ballet dancer?'

'Shouldn't think so. I expect I'll have to work in a bank too.'

'How awful!' said Lou.

Mrs Browne had managed to get them a videotape of *Petrushka*. It was about a puppet show. Petrushka was a clown who was in love with a little ballerina, only she was in love with a fierce Moor. The dancing was lovely but it was very sad and the little clown died in the end. Emma cried. She hated to see him so sad and lonely.

Mrs Dillon made a hot drink while Lou got out the biscuit tin. Mr Browne started hammering overhead, which woke up Charlie. He came out rubbing his eyes, climbed on to the sofa and settled down on Emma's lap. She cuddled him and they both seemed to be comforted.

'I have good news,' said Mrs Dillon when he was asleep again. 'Miss Maple is asking me to be a patron of the ballet school.'

'What's a patron?' asked Lou.

'Well . . .' Mrs Dillon didn't seem quite sure herself. 'It seems I am to judge competitions and give special coaching for older girls who try for the Royal Ballet School.'

'Wow!' said Lou. 'You'll be really important!'

She wondered if Mrs Dillon would judge their class at the end-of-term display. And, if so, would it help that Mrs Dillon was her friend? Would she give her better marks than Angela?

'I have more news.' Mrs Dillon hesitated. 'Perhaps you are not liking this so much.'

'Tell us,' said Lou anxiously. Suppose Mrs Dillon was too busy being a patron now to take their practice?

'I am having coffee one morning with

Mrs Sinclair.'

Lou and Emma did not know anyone by that name.

'She is asking me if her grandson can join our practice . . . but perhaps you are not liking a boy in the class?'

'A boy,' said Emma doubtfully. 'What's his name?'

'Is Jeremy, I think,' said Mrs Dillon.

'No it's not,' said Lou with a wide grin. 'It's Jerome . . . after the songwriter, not the saint.'

Emma was no wiser.

'She means Jem!' said Lou. 'He's going to join our practice! Angela will just *die* when she finds out.' Her voice rose to a high pitch with excitement.

'You will die, if you wake Charlie again,' warned Mrs Dillon. 'Does this mean that you are liking this boy to come?'

'Oh, yes, *please*,' said Lou and Emma in chorus.

'Then I shall ask your mothers if they are approving.' Mrs Dillon picked up Charlie and carried him back to bed, leaving the two girls grinning on the sofa.

Chapter Six

The invitations came on the Wednesday morning. '*ANGELA*', they said, '*is having a PARTY.*' At the bottom of each, the Wind-up Merchant had scribbled, '*Please come! It wouldn't be the same without my Rats.*'

Emma came racing downstairs. She had been invited! At last she might make some friends at school . . . But suppose Lou refused to go?

'Have you got one?' she asked breathlessly.

Lou was very laid-back about it. 'Angela's party?' she said. 'Mmm . . . I suppose we'd better go, or the Wind-up Merchant might be hurt.'

'Oh, yes!' said Emma. 'That's what I thought. I mean . . . he *is* our friend and the party *is* at his house and I expect he planned it all.'

'And he does say it won't be the same without us,' said Lou. 'Yes, I think we'd better go.'

Actually, she wanted to go almost as much as Emma did. She was curious to see where Angela lived; she knew that it was one of the big houses near the park. And she knew that if they were not there, they would have to spend weeks in the changing room, listening to all Angela's friends going on about how WONDERFUL it had been.

Emma set off to school in high spirits . . . but she came home in tears.

'Angela was really horrible to me when I tried to thank her for the invitation,' she

sobbed in Lou's room. 'She turned to her friends and said that it was her grandfather who'd invited me (*sob, sob*) and that *she* would be too proud to go to a party (*snuffle, snuffle*) if she hadn't been invited (*sniff, sniff*) by the person whose birthday it was (*sob*), and then all her friends looked at me as if I was rubbish.'

Lou hugged her, and Charlie, who hated to see anyone crying, gave her some of his rather messy kisses. 'That girl is the *pits*,' said Lou. 'Just wait till I see her at ballet class!'

'I don't think I'll go tonight,' said Emma, blowing her nose. 'I'll tell my mum I've got a headache . . . Well, I have anyway.'

Lou did not try to change her mind. She thought it would be better if Emma

was not there. Emma did not like to see
people quarrel.

Lou went storming into the changing
room with a face like thunder.

'You', she said to Angela, 'are a mean-
minded little PIG . . . No, you're not,
because pigs are nicer than you . . . You
are a rotten BULLY. You pick on Emma
because she's shy and kind and you know
she won't hit back.'

A terrible silence had fallen over the
room. The young ones clutched at their
mothers and gazed at Lou with open
mouths. One mother snatched up her
little darling and covered her ears. Angela
flushed bright red and her friends stared
at Lou in horror.

'And if you think Emma and me want

to come to your stupid party, you're wrong!' shouted Lou. 'We wouldn't be seen *dead* at it.' She held out the invitations, tore them into shreds and threw the scraps in a heap at Angela's feet. Then she stormed out again.

Once in the quiet corridor, she could hear her heart beating. She dived into the studio where she found Jem on his own,

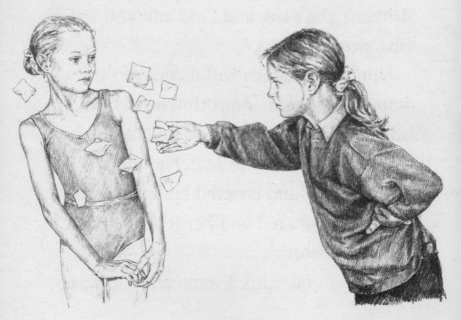

idly tinkling at the piano. He took one look at her face and said, 'Wow! What happened?'

'Don't ask!' shouted Lou, who had just realized that she had not changed yet. She could not go back. 'Just play the piano,' she said, 'and don't turn round. I have to get my things on.'

Everything went wrong. She got her tights in a twist and her leotard on backwards.

Jem listened to her little cries of despair and said, 'Do you want some help?' His voice was full of laughter.

'No, I don't!' she yelled. 'And don't turn round!' She was back to her knickers and getting desperate. The others would come in at any moment and she would look such a FOOL!

51

At last she got it right and said, 'OK, you can turn round now.'

Jem looked her up and down. 'Hmm,' he said, 'I don't think Mrs Dennison will be keen on that hairstyle.'

Lou clutched at her hair, which she had quite forgotten. She and Emma usually did each other's. Frantically she wound it about, but her fingers had all turned into thumbs. Each time, one lock of hair fell out at the last moment.

'Come here, I'll have a go,' said Jem calmly, when she was almost in tears. He sat her on the piano stool, wound her hair into a neat bun and snapped the little blue bun-net over it. He was just sticking in her hairpins when the door opened and Angela and the others came in . . .

*

'It was brilliant,' Lou told Emma when she got home. 'You should have seen the look on her face! I think she minded more when she saw Jem fixing my hair than she did when I yelled at her.'

But she did not tell Emma about her talk with Jem on the way home. He had wanted to know what it was all about, and Lou had jumped at the chance to tell him what Angela was really like, pouring out the whole story of the bullying and Emma's tears . . . And now she felt really guilty. What Emma had told her was private; she was not supposed to tell anyone else. And Lou had no excuse. After all, it wasn't as if Jem could *do* anything about it.

Chapter Seven

On Friday morning a letter arrived for
Emma. It said:

Dear Emma
Please come to my birthday party. I
would really like you to come. I am
sorry if I was mean to you. Please
make Lucy come too.
From Angela

Emma could hardly believe it. She raced

downstairs and met Lou on her way up. Lou read from the note she held in her hand:

Dear Lucy
Please come to my birthday party. I would really like you to come. I am sorry if I was mean to Emma. Please make her come too.
From Angela

'What is she up to now?' she said. 'Her grandfather must have made her write these.'

'Do you think so?' asked Emma. She had been hoping that Lou's telling-off had suddenly changed Angela into a really nice person. 'I suppose you're right,' she sighed. 'So, do you think we should go?'

'Let's see how she treats you at school today,' said Lou wisely.

When Emma got home, Lou was waiting.

'Was she nice to you?'

'Well . . . yes . . .' said Emma,

'only . . . she was sort of *too* nice . . . I mean, as if she was *acting* a nice person.'

Lou snorted. 'She's up to something,' she said. 'Maybe the Wind-up Merchant said he would cancel the party if we didn't come.'

'Why would he do that?' asked Emma. 'She's his granddaughter and he's bound to be fond of her.'

'True . . .' said Lou. 'It does seem a bit odd. Maybe he's winding *her* up. Maybe he *said* he would stop the party . . . but he wouldn't really.'

'It *was* better at school,' said Emma wistfully. 'I mean . . . her friends were nicer to me. They asked me to sit at their table at lunchtime.' And yet she remembered how uncomfortable she had felt . . . the pretend politeness, the secret smiles. It was better than being ignored, but not *much* better.

It was Jenny Lambert's evening class that night, when Mrs Dillon came to babysit Charlie and gave them their practice session.

They were working hard to catch up with the rest of the class, so that they could do their first grade exam at the end of the year. Each week Mrs Dennison wrote in a little notebook the steps they were to practise, and Mrs Dillon made sure that they did them properly.

And now Jem was to join them.

'We will have no nonsense because this boy is coming,' warned Mrs Dillon. 'We will not have gigglies or showing off.'

Lou and Emma were shocked.

'Gigglies!' they protested. 'Showing off! Of course we won't!' And they both giggled.

'Do your giggling before the boy comes,' advised Mrs Dillon. 'Once he is here, we will have discipline!'

When Jem arrived she was very stern, which made him strangely shy and a bit nervous. Lou and Emma saw that he treated the old lady with great respect, listening carefully when she corrected his movements. This made them behave themselves and take the practice session very seriously. It was, as Lou said afterwards, 'all a bit heavy' until Charlie woke up.

As the ballet practice neared its end, they suddenly heard him, banging on his cot and calling, 'Lou! . . . Lou! . . .

Bottom want Lou!'

This made it impossible not to giggle. Even Mrs Dillon laughed. 'We will have your *révérences* now,' she said, 'and then we will be seeing what that young man is up to.'

As Lou curtsied, with Jem bowing beside her, she pretended that they were on the stage at the Opera House. She imagined how he would one day take her hand and present her to the audience, making it clear that she

was the real star. The audience would
shout for her, 'Lou! Lou!'

Jem waved his fingers in front of her
eyes. The vision faded; she was back in
Emma's bedroom and Charlie was
beginning to wail.

They did not watch a video that night,
but Jem stayed for a drink and talked to
Mrs Dillon about the days when she had
been Irina Barashkova and danced with
the Bolshoi. Lou and Emma sat side by
side on the sofa listening to them, while
Charlie dozed across both their laps.
When he was asleep, Mrs Dillon put him
back in his cot and the two girls went out
on to the steps to see Jem on his way. It
was a cold night, clear and windless, with
stars.

Jem wheeled his bike to the foot of the

steps. Looking up at them he said, 'Are you two going to Angela's party then?'

'We haven't decided,' said Lou. 'We might and we might not.'

'Well, let me know,' he said, 'because she's invited me too.' And with that he waved and rode off into the night.

Chapter Eight

All the girls at school were talking about it. Someone knew someone who had seen Jem coming out of Angela's house last Wednesday evening.

'That Angela is his girlfriend,' Melanie told them. 'But she's really snobby and horrible.'

'Well, if you're pretty and you've got lots of money, you don't have to be nice as well,' said Tracey bitterly.

Lou said nothing; she was too angry. The very evening when she had told him how Angela was bullying Emma! He had gone to see her . . . at her house . . . He was even going to her party!

'Lots of money *and* a big, posh house,' said Liza.

They all agreed that boys were the pits.

On the way home, Jem rode ahead with a gang of boys. They looked as though they were teasing him, but he didn't seem to mind. At the corner of her street, Lou found him alone, waiting for her.

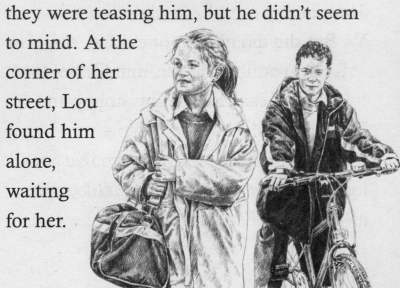

'Hi!' he said.

Lou looked at him coldly and walked on without stopping. He rode beside her.

'You're coming to our house tonight,' he said. 'For supper . . . all of you . . .'

Lou had almost forgotten. It was Jem's gran's Caribbean night.

'I may not come,' she said. 'I've got a bad headache,' and she turned away down her basement steps without asking him in.

But she did go. For one thing, she was curious about his home, and for another, she hoped it would annoy Angela to know that she had been there.

Jem's grandad was nice. He had long grey hair tied back in a ponytail, a soft Scottish accent and freckles. He was not at all like Jem except that they were both tall and slim.

The house was full of warmth and colour and music. The food was strange and delicious. Everyone had been invited: the Brownes, the Lamberts and Mrs Dillon. Even Charlie had come along to join the fun. It should have been a wonderful evening, and so it was . . . for everyone except Lou.

Jem asked about her headache. He could

see that she was not in a good mood.

'Headache?' said Jenny, catching the word. 'I didn't know you had a headache, Lou. You should have said.' And then everyone clucked over her. He did that on purpose, she thought furiously, just to show me up. Jem caught her frosty glare, so he went and talked to Emma. And then he went on talking to Emma – all evening. Lou got quite fed up with watching the pair of them jabbering away. Emma was supposed to be her friend. It was true that she did come over and ask if Lou was all right. But Lou couldn't tell her about Jem and Angela, so she just said, 'I'm OK. I don't feel like talking, that's all.'

'I expect you're getting that flu thing,' said Emma kindly. 'I mean, with your headache and everything. You don't look very well.'

Thanks a lot! thought Lou crossly. Not only is everyone ignoring me, but I look awful too! But aloud she just growled, 'Go and talk to Jem . . .' And Emma did.

After supper, they made music. Jem's grandad, whose name was John, played the piano and his gran, Aurelia, known as Orly, was persuaded to sing. Her voice was deep and rich like treacle toffee, but she could also sing high and clear. Then Mrs Dillon announced that she would sing a Russian folk-song. Jem's grandad knew the tune and played for her. The song was slow and tuneful but rather gloomy. Afterwards John played them something a bit livelier on his clarinet.

Then Jem and Emma found that they

both knew the same piano piece and
played it as a rather wobbly duet. They
were not very good but they got a lot of
applause. So Charlie had a go, plonking
up and down the keys and being
rewarded with lots of kisses. Lou felt
really left out. The others smiled at her
kindly from time to time. They all
thought she was being brave about her
headache so as not to spoil the fun. In the
end, she really did have a headache. She
was glad when it was time to go home.

Emma came to say goodnight.

'What were you and Jem chattering
about all evening?' asked Lou.

'He was telling me about his mother,'
said Emma.

'So, where is she then?'

'She's in Germany,' said Emma. 'She sings with a group. She travels a lot because of her career. But Jem says he doesn't mind because he's always lived with his gran and grandad.'

Lou really hated it when Emma knew things *she* didn't know.

'Oh, well then,' she said. 'That's all right then, isn't it?'

She sounded irritable and Emma looked at her anxiously. 'I hope you haven't got flu,' she said, 'or we'll miss Angela's party.'

'You could always go with Jem,' said Lou bitterly.

Emma looked shocked. 'Oh, no!' she said. 'I would never go without you!'

Lou felt a bit better.

Chapter Nine

'Does Angela live with her grandfather?'
asked Mrs Browne. She was driving Lou
and Emma to the party.

'Yes,' said Emma. 'Her grandmother
died a few years ago, so Angela's mother
runs the house.'

'What about her father?'

'He left home when Angela was quite
small,' said Emma.

'Oh, how sad!' said Mrs Browne.

Now Emma even knew things about *Angela* that Lou didn't know. It was very annoying . . .

'This must be it,' said Mrs Browne. 'What a lovely house!' She parked at the foot of the elegant steps and the girls jumped out. 'Have a good time,' she called as she drove off.

'Fat chance!' said Lou, who wasn't looking forward to watching Angela swanning about and showing off.

But Emma was starry-eyed. 'Oh, Lou!' she said. 'I'm sure it's going to be fun!'

The front door stood open and they could hear shrieks of laughter. A young woman greeted them and took their coats.

The noise was coming from the back of the house, where a bouncy castle had

been set up. It wasn't big enough for
everyone, so her friends were watching
while Angela jumped up and down. With
her was Jem and *three other boys from Lou's
school*! Lou was outraged; this was

poaching of the worst kind!

Angela looked as though she was having a great time. Her face was flushed and her blonde hair was flying. She seemed to go out of her way to bump into Jem and he didn't seem to mind. Angela's friends greeted Emma with sugary sweetness; they ignored Lou.

This is going to be too awful, she thought. Maybe I could sneak off home when no one is looking.

She felt a hand on her shoulder and, turning, saw Angela's grandfather. He beckoned her into a book-lined room.

'I need some help from my favourite Rat,' he said. 'I'm doing some magic tricks after tea and Angela was going to help me. Now she says she won't do it. She wants to stay with her new friend –

some boy, I think – so I need a new
assistant.'

'Oh, great!' said Lou. Now it wouldn't
be boring. 'What will I have to do?' she
asked eagerly.

'Just hand me some props,' said the
Wind-up Merchant, 'look after the rabbits
I pull out of hats . . . oh, and at the end I
make you disappear.'

'Disappear!' said Lou. 'Is this a wind-
up?'

Angela's grandfather laughed. 'Cross
my heart,' he said. 'I've hired a real
vanishing cabinet.'

'Brilliant!' said Lou. 'I don't suppose
there's a costume too?'

'Chosen for Angela, so it should fit
you. I've got robes and a turban and
you've got . . .'

'Veils and things?' said Lou eagerly.

'Got it in one!' said the Wind-up Merchant.

A tall, very thin woman came in. Lou could see at once that she was Angela's mother. 'Will she do it?' the woman asked.

'Oh, yes!' said Lou. 'I mean . . . I really love magic.'

'How kind,' said the woman without enthusiasm. 'Maria will bring you to my room after tea and I will help you dress.' She smiled politely and went out again.

'We'll need a rehearsal,' said the Wind-up Merchant. 'Do you mind missing the bouncy castle?'

'Oh, no!' said Lou. 'I think they're a bit childish.'

They practised all the tricks, including

the marvellous vanishing cabinet. The
rabbit wasn't real but you could make its
ears wiggle. Lou decided to be the best
magic assistant ever.

There was a splendid tea and Emma
came to sit next to her. 'Where have you
been?' she asked. 'I couldn't find you
anywhere.'

'It's a secret,' said Lou. 'You'll find out
later.'

She felt a bit mean, but Emma *had* left
her for her new schoolfriends. After tea
the others went to watch cartoons on a
huge video screen.

Maria, the young woman who had
taken their coats, appeared from nowhere
and led Lou up to a luxurious bedroom
where Angela's mother was waiting. The

costume was fabulous: harem pants, embroidered slippers with turned-up toes and a top decorated with shining beads. There was even a jewelled headdress and a veil which showed only her eyes. Angela's mother added some eye make-up.

There were pictures in Lou's ballet book of a dancer in a costume just like it. Lou longed to dance in it.

'Perfect,' said the Wind-up Merchant when he saw her.

'You look pretty good too,' said Lou, admiring his magician's robes and the turban with a huge jewel in it.

The magic had been set up in another room with special coloured lighting. The audience sat on the thick carpet. There was Eastern music and Lou appeared in a puff of smoke when the Magician waved his hand. Everyone gasped and Lou got carried away. She improvised a swaying dance and the audience clapped and cheered.

'You're upstaging me again,' hissed the Magician, but Lou could see that he was laughing. She went a bit over the top, dancing on and off with the props and making the rabbit's ears wiggle like mad. The vanishing cabinet was a great success, with Lou disappearing and reappearing in puffs of coloured smoke.

The applause at the end was deafening. The Magician waved his hand in front of Lou's face and removed her veil so that they could see who it was. Jem was clapping as hard as he could, while Angela sat stony-faced beside him, her hands hardly moving at all. Serve her right, thought Lou, for letting her grandfather down.

There was a disco after the magic. Lou wished she could keep the costume on, but it was only hired and a bit fragile for disco-dancing. But even in her own clothes she found herself the centre of attention. Jem danced with Angela but the others clustered around Lou. They wanted to know how the tricks were done, but Lou had promised not to tell.

The party ended with fireworks in the garden. They watched from the terrace but it was spoilt for Lou when every burst of light and colour showed Jem still right by Angela's side. I don't care. I don't *care*! Lou told herself. If he is stupid enough to want to be Angela's friend, she can jolly well have him!

Chapter Ten

The next day seemed very dull. It was Sunday and Emma had gone with her parents to visit her granny in Worthing. Jenny was busy with her evening-class homework, Charlie was having his afternoon nap and Lou was really bored. There was a knock at the door.

'Get that, will you, Lou?' called Jenny.

It was Jem.

Lou glared at him. 'Angela let you off

your lead, has she?' she said frostily.

'Don't be like that, Lou,' said Jem. 'Do you want to come down to the park?'

Lou did, but she was also pretty angry with him. She wavered for a minute, then called, 'I'm going to the park with Jem, Mum.'

'Be back by four,' called her mother.

As they went Jem said, 'The magic was great. I really like Angela's grandad.'

'So do I,' said Lou.

'You looked great,' said Jem.

'With a veil over my face, you mean?'

Jem laughed. 'With or without,' he said.

The park was cold and deserted. Lou sat on the damp roundabout while Jem pushed it round.

'I did a deal with Angela', he said, 'after you told me about Emma.'

Lou said nothing.

'I told her I would only go to her party if you and Emma were there . . .'

Still Lou said nothing.

'And that if they were nice to Em at school, I would bring three other boys to the party with me.'

'You sold out,' said Lou coldly.

'Well . . . sort of,' said Jem cheerfully, 'and she drove a hard bargain! She made me promise to stay next to her all through the party.'

'You're pathetic,' said Lou.

'But it worked,' said Jem. 'It worked better than you yelling at her. Em had a great time and the others are getting to know her.'

'It won't last,' said Lou.

'Maybe . . . Maybe not.'

As they walked back, Jem said, 'There's worse that I haven't told you.'

Lou wasn't sure that she wanted to hear.

'I didn't just do it for Emma,' he said. 'It was for me too. Everyone knows that

Angela has amazing parties and the other boys all wanted to go. They think she's great. I was the one who could get them invited. I was the one she talked to all evening. It made me look good.'

'You slimeball!' said Lou, grinning.

'Aren't I just!' He grinned back. 'A boy who does ballet', he explained, 'has to work hard at his image!'

'You mean he needs to be friends with the most popular girl?'

'It helps.'

There was a long silence.

'So why are you here?' asked Lou. 'Why aren't you round at Angela's?'

'Ah, well,' said Jem. 'It was your magic dancing. The others think you're the flavour of the month now . . .'

He ducked as she went to hit him and

she had to chase him the rest of the way
home.

But she hadn't quite forgiven him. He
shouldn't have done it without her
knowing. She needed to talk about it and
she couldn't tell Emma. So that night

when she went to bed, she told her mother.

'It was kind of him to want to help Emma,' said Jenny.

'He did it for himself too!'

'We all do things for ourselves.'

'But he should have told *me* what he was doing! I mean, Emma is *my* friend.'

'She is his friend too.'

There was a long silence. Then her mother said, 'Friendship is a sort of network, Lou. It links us all to one another. But a net is not a web with one person in the centre, knowing what all the others do, pulling all the strings.'

'But, Mum, the others . . . they're not really Emma's friends,' protested Lou. 'Not like I am. They just pretend to be nice to her when Angela tells them to.'

'Do you think Emma doesn't know that? Do you think she can't tell real friends from fake ones?'

Lou thought about it. She knew how badly Emma wanted to fit in at school. She might want it enough to fool herself. Suppose she settled for being one of Angela's cronies? Lou sighed. But her mother was right about the web. That was just the sort of friendship Angela offered. She sat in the centre of her web like a rich, fat spider. When she moved, the whole web shook and all her friends jumped about. And now she had fixed her sticky little threads on to Emma and Jem and she was starting to reel them in . . .

Lou really liked this image. She pictured Angela's face on a little fat body with lots of legs sticking out . . .

Well, she won't get me, she thought.
And she won't get Jem and Emma, not if
I can help it . . . But she didn't know
what she was going to do about it.

'Maybe you just have to trust Emma,'
said Jenny, as if she read Lou's thoughts.
'I think you will always be her best
friend.'

She hugged Lou and kissed her
goodnight. Lou hugged her back. As she
snuggled down under her quilt, her
mother paused in the doorway. 'And that
boy isn't stupid,' she said. 'I think he can
tell who his real friends are.' Then she
switched out the light.

Lou dozed in the dark and thought
about it. She wasn't so sure . . . about
Jem not being stupid . . . After all, he

did say he might decide to become a
footballer . . . She would have to stay
friends with him, just to make sure he
didn't . . . He was such a good dancer
. . . and ballet needed all the boys it
could get.

Dancing Shoes

Hi!

Well, so much has happened since I last wrote – Emma and I thought we should tell you all our news!

Imagine, a boy in our ballet class. What a surprise! Jem is such a good dancer, and luckily for Emma and me he is a good friend too. Now all three of us will practise our ballet together and we'll work even harder. I am going to try to be just as good at ballet as Angela – maybe even better!

I hope Angela's going to start being a bit nicer to Emma at school (she's always so horrible). But even Angela can't spoil ballet classes for me and Emma. We love them!

Love

Lou

PS Catch up with Emma and me in DANCING SHOES: OUT OF STEP.